This
Little Princess Story
belongs to:

....

To my little
PRINCESS
ELIZABETH
for your
Birthday!
4 today!
EAH!
Lots of
love,

Mama
XXXXXXOᴑᴑᴑ
28/10/2014

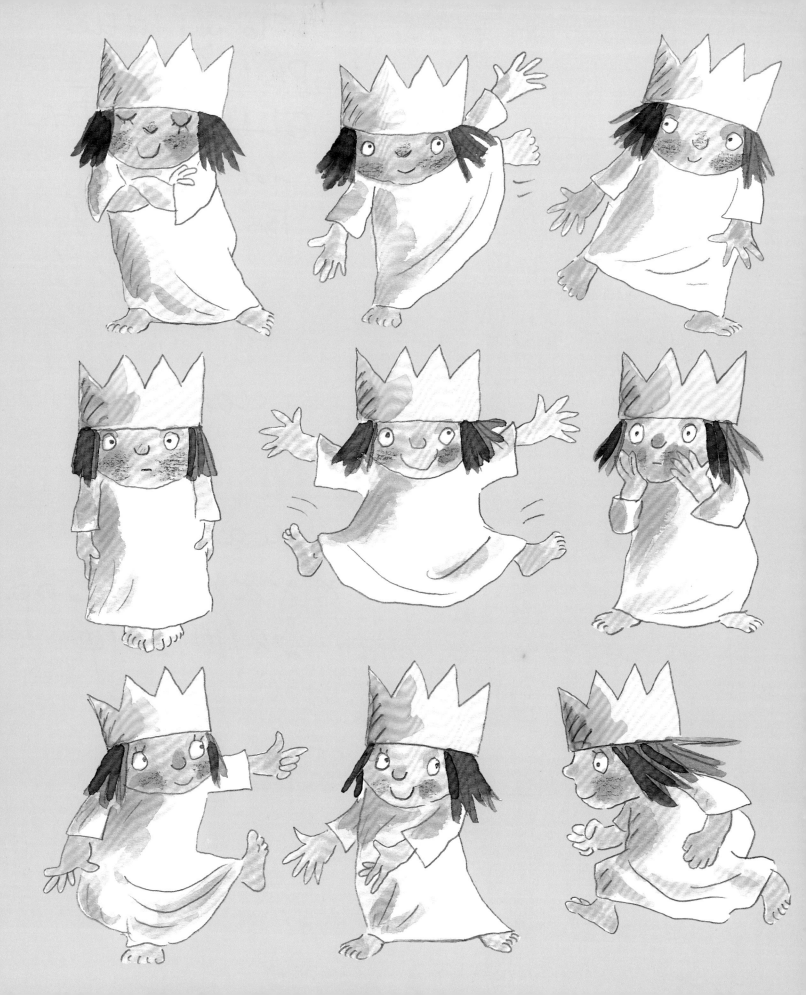

To Beth, who liked hospital

This paperback edition first published in 2010 by Andersen Press Ltd.

First published in Great Britain in 2000 by Andersen Press Ltd., 20 Vauxhall Bridge Road, London SW1V 2SA.

Published in Australia by Random House Australia Pty., Level 3, 100 Pacific Highway, North Sydney, NSW 2060.

Copyright © Tony Ross, 2000

Colour separated in Switzerland by Photolitho AG, Zürich.

Printed and bound in China by Foshan Zhao Rong Printing Co., Ltd.

10   9   8   7   6   5   4   3   2

British Library Cataloguing in Publication Data available.

ISBN 978 1 84939 024 8 (Trade paperback edition)

ISBN 978 1 78344 021 4 (Riverside edition)

A Little Princess Story

I Don't Want to Go to Hospital!

Tony Ross

Andersen Press

"Ooo, Oww, Ooo," cried the Little Princess.
"My nose hurts!"

"You've got a little lump up there," said the Doctor.

"I'll get it out," said the General, drawing his sword.

"No," said the Doctor, "it won't come out.
Her Majesty must go to hospital."

"No!" cried the Princess. "I don't want to go to hospital!"

"It's nice in hospital," said the Doctor. "You'll get sweets and cards."
"I don't want to go," said the Princess.

"It's nice in hospital," said the Queen, who had been there.
"I don't want to go," said the Princess.

"You'll meet lots of new friends in hospital,"
said the Prime Minister.

"No! I don't WANT to go to hospital!" said the Princess,
and she ran out of the room.

"Where is the Princess?" cried the Queen.
"It's time to go."

"She's not in her room," said the Maid.

"She's not in the dustbin," said the Cook.

"She's not in any of my boats," said the Admiral.

"She's not on the roof," said the Gardener.

"She's in the attic!" said the King.
"I don't want to go to hospital," said the Princess.

But the Little Princess had to go.

And the lump came out of her nose.

"Now you are better," said the Queen, "you can brush
your teeth, and comb your hair . . .

. . . and tidy your room, and . . ."
"No!" cried the Princess . . .

". . . I want my tonsils out!"

"But why?" said the Queen.
"I want to go back to hospital," said the Little Princess.

"They treated me like a Princess in there."

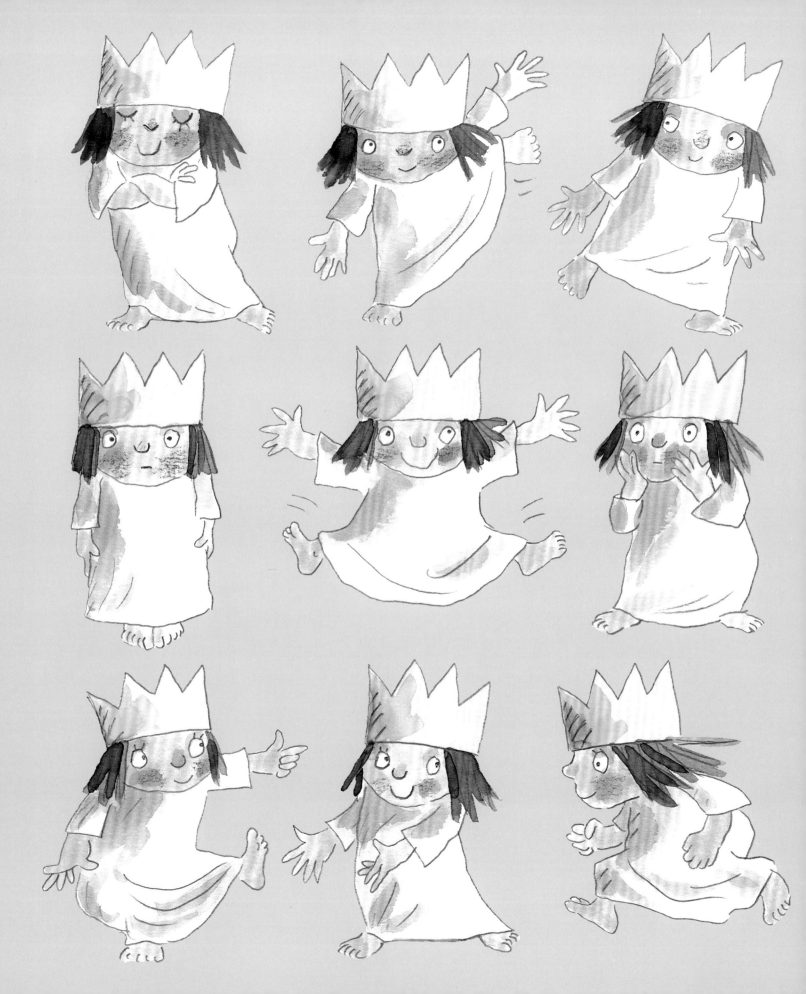

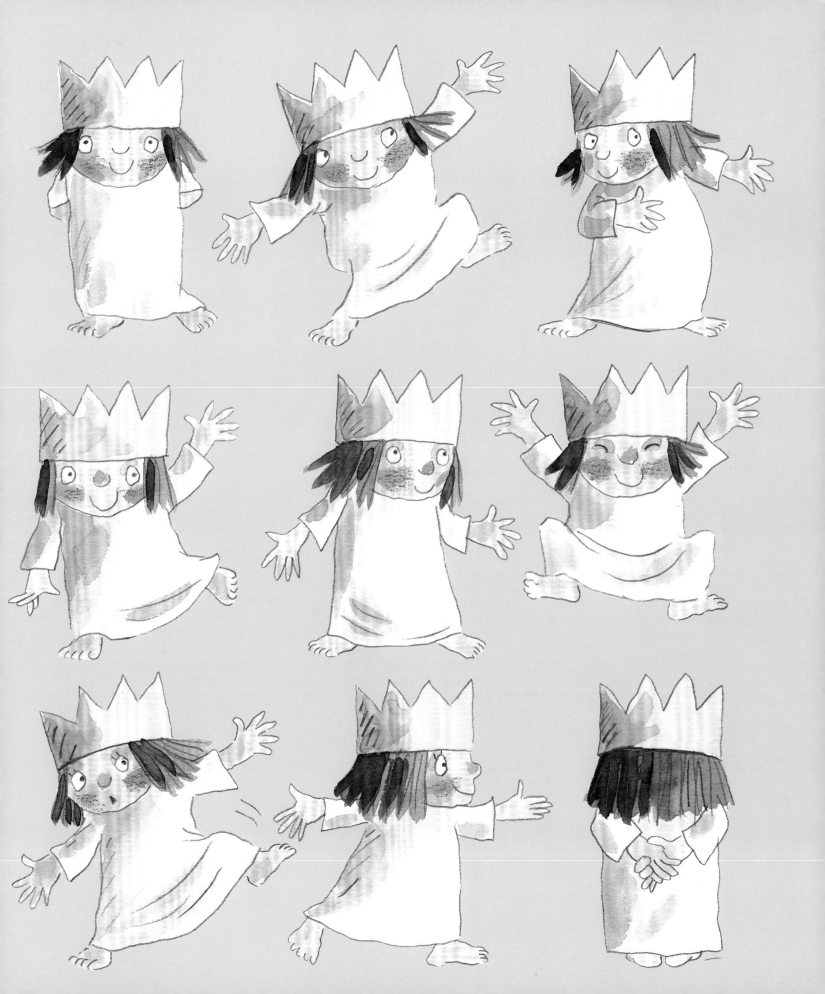

Other Little Princess Books

Little Princess titles are also available as eBooks.